In Memory of
Maddy

Amy K. Barham

PublishAmerica
Baltimore

First printing

ISBN: 1-4137-8279-5
PUBLISHED BY PUBLISHAMERICA, LLLP
www.publishamerica.com
Baltimore

Printed in the United States of America

To my two precious daughters,
Chelsey Lynn and
Tressa Camille Barham
May all of your dreams come true.

Also, to my dear husband, Tracy.
I appreciate your love and support.

"There is a destiny that makes us brothers
None goes his way alone.
All that we send into
the lives of others
Comes back into our own."
–Markham, Charles Edwin

Part I

Chapter 1

December 4, 1947

An angelic melody flowed from the chipped crystal trinket box that sat upon the weathered vanity table in the corner of Maddy's bedroom.

She spun around gracefully as her feet twirled in the air. So special, so free she felt as she danced around and around. Her golden-blonde hair had fallen from her braid and feathered innocently across her baby blue eyes.

Maddy imagined that she was a beautiful princess held captive in an extravagant castle of any ten-year- old's fairytale.

The dingy, yellow wallpaper with little blue flowers that sagged from her bedroom walls magically transformed into walls that were lavishly decorated with intricate flowers of a soft, velvet design.

The cracked, stained ceiling above stood imaginatively taller and was artistically framed with etched, white crown molding.

An elegant glass chandelier would replace her plain, white light bulb that carelessly dangled exposing the black and red electrical wires.

Slowly the music box played as it unwound. In step, Maddy slowly sauntered toward the ground.

She sat, bent over with her arms stretched forth.

Ever so gently she welcomed the silence. She lifted her head and offered her imaginary audience a warm, gracious smile.

It was at that moment that she heard the clapping. Still dazed by the reeling effect from her dance, Maddy was unsure if the applause was realistic or merely a figment of her imagination as the rest of the afternoon had been.

Ah, the magic of it all!

"Papa!" she squealed as she noticed him standing proudly in the doorway.

"You made it just like you said you would!" Maddy exclaimed as she ran and jumped into his opened arms.

"You are home for my birthday."

"Oh, my fair lady, home indeed, and I come bearing a special gift for you princess."

"A gift for me Papa? You shouldn't have." A mixed feeling of appreciation and guilt overcame Maddy.

Her father, Mack Murray, had been laid off his steady job at the lumberyard three months ago.

The reason given for Mack's release was his inability to comply with the customer's needs, but everyone knew that it was his excess indulgence of drink that got him fired.

He wouldn't ever drink at work, but the effects of the evenings would definitely pay their toll in the mornings. He would stroll into work late claiming that he was right on time, threatening anyone who said any different.

Mack finally found the limit that his boss, Jack Wright, would take. He had threatened to crack a board over Jack's head when he docked Mack's paycheck for all of the minutes he had been late.

Mack was blind to the real reason, of course. His boss feared him.

Standing at 5'6, Mack was not considered a huge man, but a stout man who could definitely hold his own. Jack decided that it would be best not to chance it.

Generally, Mack's eyes were an icy blue, numb from all of the pain and cold that the world around him offered.

Tonight, however, they melted as they lingered into the little girl's eyes that warmed his soul, his precious Maddy.

Hesitantly, but excitedly, she opened the gift making sure not to tear the paper.

"You are making me anxious and I know what it is. Hurry up and open it girl."

"Oh Papa, they are beautiful." Maddy lifted the shoes up out of the box.

"Happy tenth birthday, baby."

Tears filled Maddy's eyes as she slipped the shoes on her feet. She seldom received new shoes, and never, until today, did she receive red patent leather shoes.

"Papa, I do not know what to say." Maddy exclaimed as she stood with her arms crossing her chest as she looked down adoring her pretty new shoes.

"Say yes, Princess Maddy."

"Yes to what, Prince Papa?"

"Yes that you will allow me a dance with your new magical slippers."

Mack then wound the crystal music box as tight as it would turn. He then faced Maddy and took her delicate hand. Upon it, he placed a loving, fatherly kiss.

"May I, dear Maddy, have this dance?"

"Oh Papa, yes!" Maddy cried with such delight.

Mack embraced his daughter securely in his arms.

Together they waltzed to the tune, twisting and swaying their way back into Maddy's fairytale.

The sound of her music box shattering into a million pieces on the cold hardwood floor below quickly surfaced them both back to reality.

Chapter 2

Maddy knew what had happened before she even looked up. "Her name is Madison Grace, named after my mother, God bless her. Not Mm-a-d-dy!" Maddy felt herself cringe as her father's pet name for her rolled carelessly off of her mother's tongue.

Patricia had once been a beautiful woman. Maddy would never have believed it had she not seen her mother's wedding pictures for herself.

The auburn shoulder length curls that she wore as a bride were now a dull brown with course gray strands peeping through.

Patricia's rosy cheeks and plush pink lips of her youth had been replaced with weathered wrinkles and her mouth coarse and cracked.

The vibrant shine in her eyes had been long exchanged for the bitter glare that she offered Mack and Maddy at this moment.

"What in God's creation do you two think you are doing?" Patricia posed with both of her hands on her hips as her eyes darted back and forth between Mack and Maddy.

Maddy slowly stopped behind her father and wrapped her arms around his right leg, hoping that his large stature would shield her from her mother's evil wrath.

Her left foot naively slipped between her father's stance exposing one shiny red patent leather slipper.

"Well, well, well." Patricia's grueling expression was immediately exchanged for a vengeful smirk.

"My baby has new shoes for her birthday, does she? While your brother and I are in the kitchen trying to scrape up food to eat, you and your daddy are in here playing these nonsense games."

Mack stood silently clenching his jaws and balling his fingers into fist. This was not his wife's first angry outburst toward Maddy or himself. He knew exactly where her anger was directed and be damned if he would let her reach his baby girl.

"Madison, darling, give momma the shoes. We can't afford them because of your sorry son-of-a..."

Heat penetrated through Mack's hand leaving a tingling sensation. Patricia stood with her mouth agape, her palm cradling her red cheek.

She was in awe. Mack had never raised his voice to her, much less a hand. He would generally cower with his face to the ground until she vented her rage.

"You, you." no names came to mind that could describe the way that she felt about Mack at this particular moment.

"Woman, you never degrade me in front of my children again! Do you understand?" Mack stood firm and unmoved as he caught Patricia's wrist with one hand as she tried to retaliate.

Mack then twisted Patricia's helpless arm behind her back.

"Calm down, then I will let you go." Mack ordered.

Patricia unsuccessfully struggled to free herself.

"I am not going to hurt you, Trish. Calm down."

Like a wild animal, Patricia fought until pure exhaustion overtook her.

Her eyes shallow and her face pale, she finally gave in and her breathing, loud and deep, began to slow down.

Mack released his firm grip and stared at Patricia as she rubbed her aching wrist.

"O-kay Mack. I will be sensible. Just tell me where you got the money."

Maddy had been forgotten as she huddled in the corner of her room. She hugged her knees tightly as she could wishing that she could make herself disappear.

"It's our daughter's birthday, for heaven's sake! Can we not celebrate?"

"You have a son in the other room Mack. What about him, huh?"

"What about him? It is Maddy's birthday. What does it matter?"

"It matters Mack, oh it matters. We have done without for three whole months. I want to know, where did you get the money?"

Mack seemed troubled all of a sudden. He turned his eyes and searched for Maddy's.

His lips quivered as he painfully presented her a distressed smile.

Maddy gently smiled back and encouraged her father the strength that he needed to proceed.

Mack then turned back and faced Patricia hoping that Maddy overlooked the tears that threatened his eyes.

"I-I got the money," Mack slowly began. "I got the money," he continued.

Maddy, feeling the anticipation lifted up to sit on her knees.

"You got a job! I am so sorry that I doubted you." Relief, as well as a refreshing smile, spread across Patricia's face.

" No Trish," Mack looked into her eyes for a glint of sympathy, but none was to be found.

"Trish, I sold your wedding ring." He began to say, "I thought this is what you would want." Patricia fell limp onto the floor.

No argument, no threats or accusations. Merely death wrenching silence as Patricia stared up at Mack.

Maddy was taken aback. She was at a loss of what to do.

The pitter-patter of her patent shoes across the hardwood floor reverberated throughout the house as she ran desperately to the front door.

The sound of her little brother, Willie, wailing seemed to follow her in the wind.

She ran faster and faster towards the setting sun.

Chapter 3

"You sold my wedding ring?" Patricia calmly asked to confirm that she had heard her husband correctly.

Mack stalled answering her hoping that silence would ease the tension.

"Well, answer me." Patricia demanded.

"I told you." Mack began. "Today is Maddy's special day. I didn't have any other way. Have you become that cold-hearted to not even try and understand?"

Patricia stood up slowly. She stared right through Mack. It was as though she had transformed into someone else.

"You're right. I don't understand. Seeing that I don't have a wedding ring, I feel that I no longer belong here."

Patricia then turned and walked to the bedroom that she and Mack share. The door closed behind her. She knelt down on her knees and pulled a black, dusty suitcase out from under the bed.

The suitcase had been a wedding gift from her mother. She thought that giving Patricia the luggage would give her the incentive to come back home.

Patricia unlocked the golden latches for the first time in ten years. She lifted open the suitcase. Tears fell from her eyes as the memories that she had carefully packed away in her mind sprang forth.

Her family live on a farm in Kansas. In 1935, a severe dust storm whirled over the land diminishing most of the good top soil. The farm's crops were destroyed. No relief was to be found.

Most farmers that were still burdened by the effects of the Depression packed up and left their farms. Not William Mark Sullivan, Patricia's daddy. He was a hard working man with stubborn determination that drove him forward with a passion.

He had taken on migrant workers against her mother's disapproval.

Men, women, and children were brought in by trucks to work. With much effort, William thought that the farm could be spared. He and his family roughed it out during the Depression. Surely this couldn't be any worse.

If he would have only known that his only daughter would vow her love to one of the workers, he probably would have chosen to lose the farm of his inheritance instead.

In 1936, 17 year old Mack Murray had promised 15 year old Patricia Sullivan the light to her dismal world. She would secretly meet him under the large pecan tree that sat cozily upon the hill.

Mack had entertained Patricia by telling her of his intriguing travels. He had a dream to manage his own farm one day. He seemed to be headed somewhere promising, somewhere more generous than the barren Kansas land that she had been born.

Patricia will never forget the day she told her mother she was marrying Mack. She had waited until both of her brothers and her father were working on the far side of the field.

Her mother was in the sultry kitchen kneading dough for an apple pie. The twinkle in her mother's eyes quickly turned into devastating tears as she told her that she was leaving.

"Please Patricia, no!" Her mother pleaded, as though Patricia had a choice. Patricia had waited until she was positive she was pregnant, hoping to spare the pain.

When she was definite of her condition, she had asked Mack to take her away. Her family would accept her running away much easier than they would her having an illegitimate child.

Seeing that Patricia would not change her mind, her mother gave her the suitcase and a purple sachet of coins.

"It's not much," she claimed, "but it's all that I could save since the Depression. It's a guarantee that if things don't work out as you plan, you can at least get a train ride home."

Patricia left her home, her heritage, and her family that day. She had never looked back.

She and Mack were married that evening in a small saloon by a drunken minister that wished them well. He even took a snapshot for 5 cents so she could always remember her "special day," so he called it.

Within the next seven months, they had moved three times in Kansas in order for Mack to find work. Times were hard and jobs were scarce.

Patricia gave birth to a six pound three ounce baby girl, whom she named Madison Grace after her mother. She promised to never reveal Madison to her family in fear that it would tell of the rebellion and shame that she had brought upon them. She vowed to never return.

Within the next four years, they moved to Arkansas, Oklahoma, and then to Texas where they remain. Mack finally found a secure job at Wright's Lumber.

John Willie Murray, Willie, was born one year after he started working in the lumber yard. Mack decided to settle. Moving had exhausted them.

It occurred to Patricia that ever since she had met Mack, she has been on the run. Mack had good intentions, but he was a dreamer. A schemer of life. The most income that he had ever made had been when he was working at her Daddy's farm.

Patricia closed the tightly stuffed suitcase that held her and Willie's clothes and personal belongings. She grasped the sachet tightly in her hand. "Momma, I am coming home."

Chapter 4

Maddy ran as fast as her red patent leather shoes would take her. The sun was fading, and the winter winds began to blow. The cool and dampness of the air threatened.

Maddy continued to run. Fallen tears swept off of her face and blended with the misting rain.

She had a little hideout that would offer her security and a shield from the cold.

It was a special place that her father made for her at the lumber yard. He had set stacks of unused lumber out of the way, making Maddy a cubbyhole that she could climb in between unnoticed.

She would sing to herself, play imaginary games, and often sleep in her special place while she waited for her father to take lunch.

Mack would then sit by the lumber pile and have lunch with his little girl. They would share his sandwich, tell tales, and laugh together. Oh, how Maddy adored him.

When lunch was over, Mack would then kiss Maddy on her nose. They would vow to secrecy of their "special place." Mack would tell Maddy that it was because his employer would get upset, but Maddy knew that it was more because of her mother. Patricia would be enraged if she knew of the time that they spend together.

Maddy would then crawl back into the sweet smelling cubbyhole and wait for the five o'clock whistle to blow.

Entranced in thought, Maddy was startled by the loud whistle blowing as she stood on the train tracks that ran in front of Wright's Lumberyard.

Chapter 5

The musty, wooden house creaked as silence and darkness settled in. Two hours had passed since Patricia and Willie had walked out the door. Two hours, and Mack still sat on the cold, hardwood floor that had caught him when Patricia's venomous words knocked him off of his feet.

Now, he was all alone. Well, almost alone. Mack had pulled a small bottle of whiskey out of his boot to keep him company. His intentions were to numb the pain. Instead, the alcohol seemed only to intensify the reality of it all.

A forceful knock on the front, wooden door startled him. Again, Mack heard the persistent knock as he stumbled to make his way.

"I'm coming." He shouted in the most pleasant, and hopefully not slurred tone, that he could manage.

He ran his fingers through his hair as he reached for the doorknob. *Thank God. Trish has come to her senses.* He thought as he opened the door.

Instead of Trish, he found Jack Wright holding a brown, paper sack with both hands.

"Mack," Jack solemnly greeted, taking pity on Mack's apparent drunken condition.

"Uh, this isn't a good time, Jack." Mack replied, not caring if Jack would understand. Work was the least of his worries at the moment.

"I have something to tell you," Jack took a deep breath. "I feel that it would be better if we both sat down. May I come in?"

Curious by Jack's persistence, Mack agreed to let him in.

Jack entered the liquor tainted, dreary sitting room. He took a seat. "Please turn on a little light. I have something to show you."

Annoyed, Mack glared at Jack. "If you don't mind, can this wait? I haven't had the best of days today. Trish and Willie walked out on me, and it's Maddy's birthday. She has ran off and not came home. I'm not in the mood to talk about work!"

"I wish I were here to talk about work." Jack stated as he tried to hide the lumpin his throat that invaded his speech. "I'm here about Maddy."

"My Maddy?" Mack asked confused as he stumbled to turn on a lamp.

Jack held out the brown, paper sack that he had been clenching in his fists.

"I'm sorry."

Slowly, Mack unrolled the crinkling sack uncertain to what he might find.

"Oh, God!" Mack pleaded, as he stared down at the muddy, scratched, red patent leather shoes that she had danced in only two hours ago.

Chapter 6

Two weeks had passed since Jack Wright had paid Mack a visit to inform him that his daughter had been struck by a train. Fourteen days since Trish and Willie had walked out. They hadn't been heard from.

Mack had sent a telegram to Patricia at her parent's home in Kansas, almost certain that had been her destination. He had his doubts now since she hadn't responded to Maddy's death.

The muddy, red shoes had been carefully placed next to a black and white picture of Maddy upon the fireplace mantel.

Mack stood running his finger across the shoes. He then studied Maddy's innocent face that stared back at him.

"Baby, if only I hadn't gotten you these shoes." Tears streaked his face.

Behind him, a white letter slipped through the mail slot onto the hardwood floor. Mack bent down and picked the letter up. The return address was from Kansas.

"Finally!" Mack stated.

He pulled a timepiece out of his pocket. Two-twenty eight in the afternoon.

Mack placed the watch back into his pocket, and with it the unsealed letter from Trish.

Fierce winds wailed as Mack plodded to the funeral parlor where Maddy lay.

The gust behind him slammed the heavy entrance door announcing his arrival. Mack carefully wiped his shoes on the doormat before he stepped onto the plush, red carpet.

Mack exchanged handshakes with the funeral director, Tom Parkins, and his assistant, Gary Cooley.

Mack had frequented the parlor. His visits with Maddy was the only thing that offered him solace.

"Mr. Murray," Tom began.

Mack nodded.

"Mr. Murray, it has been two weeks since your daughter's tragedy."

Not needing to be reminded, Mack agreed.

"What Mr. Parkins is trying to say," Gary interrupted, "is that it is past time to bury your daughter."

"Mr. Cooley, I do believe that I can speak for myself!" Tom reprimanded.

"It's true, Tom. You've said so yourself." Gary replied.

"If you don't mind, Mr. Cooley, I would like to talk to Mr. Murray alone. Thank you."

Gary turned and stomped away.

"I apologize for my assistant's rude behavior." Tom said.

"He's right. I apologize if I have inconvenienced anyone."Mack said. "I have been waiting for a letter from my wife. She wasn't aware of the accident. It wouldn't be right to have her funeral without her mother."

"As you have mentioned before, Mr. Murray," Tom rubbed his neck hoping to ease the tension. "but please understand that she needs to be laid to rest."

"That is why I am here today." Mack presented the white envelope that was folded in his pocket. "I've come to tell Maddy that it came in the mail today."

"Well, by all means, go meet with Maddy." Tom excused Mack, as well as the anxiety that had built up. It had been an agonizing experience to not be able to lay this little soul to rest.

Mack entered the dense room in the parlor that Maddy lay. Mack didn't claim to be a religious man, but at this time he sure hoped that there is indeed a God watching over his baby.

The scent of lilac and roses overwhelmed him as he approached the small casket. Maddy looked so angelic as she gently rested her head on the soft, satin pillow with her blonde hair flowing freely around her face. It was almost as though a soft glow radiated from her being.

"It's here, Maddy." Mack pulled out the letter. "We will now know when we can properly lay you to rest."

His hands trembled as he opened the letter.

My Dearest Mack,

> *I apologize if my and Willie's departure has left you unstable. I have often told you to stop indulging yourself in alcohol. I do believe that drinking has made you insane, for I do not know a Maddy.*
>
> *As you are aware, Willie and I are with my parents. We are well taken care of, and do not wish for further contact from you…especially this nonsense about Maddy.*

Best Wishes,
Patricia

Tom Parkins found Mack on his knees, clenching the note in his fist and sobbing uncontrollably.

"I assume that the letter wasn't as promising as you had wished."

"No. Maddy's mother will not be attending the funeral procession." Mack replied in almost a whisper.

"I will see to all of the arrangements. Would later this afternoon be appropriate?" Tom asked.

"That would be fine." Mack replied.

Tom turned and walked away.

"Damn you, Trish, for not wanting your mother to know about Maddy." Mack wadded up the letter and tossed in the wastebasket.

Maddy was buried that evening with only Mack, Gary, and Tom attending the grave side. Snow began to fall as Tom preformed a few words of respect.

Together, they had sang, "Nearer My God To Thee." Mack knelt down and placed a single rose upon Maddy's earthen bed as Gary said a prayer of closure.

"Goodnight, sleep tight, my princess Maddy." Mack stood and walked away.

Part II

Chapter 7

May, 1977 Thirty years later.

Tick- tock. Emma watched the black, round clock hanging on the wall. Each jump that the second hand made, the tighter she would hold her books, anxious for the bell to ring.

Five, four, three, two, finally, RING!

"Emma, remain after class." Mrs. Keller's nasal quality voice droned across the classroom.

"I'll wait for you at your house." Cade mumbled as he passed Emma. Emma sat back down at her desk feeling defeated.

"As you are aware," Mrs. Keller began as she ensured that the door was completely closed for privacy, "you skimmed through the fourth grade by the skin of your teeth."

Emma sat quietly hoping that the silence would hurry the unwanted conversation along.

"I have selected a workbook for you to study over the summer."

Tick- tock and blah, blah, blah is all that Emma could focus on.

"Emma, do you have any questions?"

Emma took the workbook that Mrs. Keller was holding out to her.

"No ma'am." She turned and ran out the door leaving Mrs. Keller no choice but to end the conversation.

"Have a nice summer!" Mrs. Keller called out. Emma never turned back.

"Where have you been?" Cade asked as Emma reached the front porch completely out of breath. Emma dropped her books. She

27

doubled over and grasped both knees inhaling deep, refreshing breaths. The school was only three blocks away, but she had never ran so fast in fear that Cade would go crawdad fishing without her.

"Never mind that. You got the shoestring that I told you to bring?"

"I do."

"Well then, let me grab some bacon. Wait here." Emma gathered her books. The wooden screen door slammed behind her announcing her arrival.

"Emma Louise, is that you?" she heard her mother call. The scent of pine sol and lavender was intoxicating. "Take your shoes off."

Emma hurried back to the door and lined her shoes up along the wooden baseboard. She then skated over her dirt tracks with her white socks hoping to destroy any evidence of her forgetfulness.

The slab of bacon slid from Emma's hand as she opened the greasy wrapper. Emma picked up the glob of bacon and she shoved it in the front pocket of her denim overalls.

"Oh, Emma! You have made a mess." Her mother proclaimed as she entered the kitchen.

Emma was always making messes in Jolynn's eyes. Emma couldn't count the number of times that her mother had scolded her for "tromping dirt in the house."

"We don't live in a barn." Emma steadily wiped the grease off of the floor hoping that her mother let up on her soon.

"You should try to be more like your sister, Kate. She's at piano lessons this moment while your are standing here with the ice box wide open making a plum mess of my clean floor."

"Cade's waiting for me momma. Can I go now?"

Jolynn put each of her hands on the hip of her apron. A gentle smile spread across her face as she looked down at Emma's urgency. Emma's dark brown hair in pigtails, her pudgy cheeks, and round hazel eyes all pleaded to leave.

"How can I stay mad at you?" Jolynn claimed. "Be home before daddy gets here, and take off those dirty socks." Jolynn sang out as she returned down the hall to finish cleaning whatever that she imagined to be dirty.

Emma wadded both socks up and stuffed them into the shoes that she had lined up against the kitchen wall. She then rolled up each of her pant legs and walked barefoot onto the cemented porch.

"Ready?" Emma asked.

"I have been ready." Cade impatiently replied.

They both jumped off of the porch and headed toward the railroad tracks that sat in front of the old, abandoned lumberyard.

Chapter 8

"What did Mrs. Keller keep you so long for?"

"To wish me a good summer."

"She wouldn't have kept you for that, Emma. What's the real reason?"

"You ask too many questions Cade. It's summer and I am not thinking about school again until I absolutely have to."

Emma and Cade waved as they passed Mrs. Kitty working in her flower garden. Mrs. Kitty was always busy washing the yellow boards on her cottage home, scrubbing the porch with bubbly suds from an aluminum bucket, or wiping her windows until they glistened. She loved being outdoors in the vibrant sunshine.

"How ya'll children doin this fine day?"

"We're alright, Mrs. Kitty." Cade announced.

Mrs. Kitty wiped the sweat from her brown face.

"Lawd, hep me. Ain't even full summer yet, and here I am sweatin like a stuck pig."

She stepped out of the midst of the flowers toward Cade and Emma.

"I's fixin to sit right here and drink me a glass of lemonade. Ya'll want some?"

"No ma'am. We're on our way to go crawdad fishing by the tracks." Emma stated, hoping that she didn't sound too rude.

"Well, ya'll best be hurryin along then. Don't want to keep them crawdads awaitin."

"Do you think Mrs. Kitty's her real name?" Cade asked Emma once they were out of earshot from her.

"I don't know. Maybe she likes cats." Emma proclaimed as they walked.

"No, that can't be it. You've heard of Goat Russell haven't ya?"

"Yeah, who hasn't?"

"Well, let me tell you, He isn't named "Goat" Russell because he likes goats. Mama said it was because he never takes a bath and he wears that same old black and red checkered shirt. She said he's mean too. He gruffs and smells like an old billy goat."

"Well Cade, I don't think Mrs. Kitty smells like a cat. Maybe she has a million living in her house. Who knows?"

"Yeah, who knows?"

"She knows, I guess. She's friendly enough. Maybe you can ask her why Cade, I dare you."

"That's a dumb dare Emma."

"What, are you afraid to ask her? Scaredy cat, scaredy cat Cade."

"I ain't a scaredy cat. I can just think of better dares than that."

"Like what?" Emma asked impatiently.

"Like, well," Cade thought for a moment, "like dropping live crawdads on your momma's clean floor."

"Cade, that's a dumber dare. I make a mess all the time."

"Alright, then we can put gum in Kate's hair."

"We ain't gonna put gum in my sister's hair. That will get me grounded for the whole summer."

Cade stepped onto the railroad tracks. He reached in his denim pocket and pulled out two shiny copper pennies and placed each flat on the train rail, one for him and one for Emma.

"I've got it!" Emma shouted startling Cade.

"I dare both of us to go up to that Old Mean Mack's house."

"Are you crazy? I'd rather be grounded for the summer than killed."

Cade pulled the knotted shoestring out of his pocket and handed Emma one. They each pinched a bit of bacon that Emma had brought and tied it securely onto one end of the string. They each found a mound of mud and lowered their string down into the dark, wet hole in the center.

31

Emma squat hovering over her mound, while Cade sat indian styled, for there was nothing more to do but to hold onto the string and wait for a nibble.

"I heard that old man doesn't leave his house. He's always there, so he'll catch us snooping."

"He has to leave sometimes. He eats, doesn't he?"

"Yes, but Momma says that black boy, Arnold, at Mr. Druthers's Grocery store, delivers food to him. Old Mean Mack orders them on the phone."

"Your momma knows too much about other people's business, Cade. Just because she says it doesn't mean that it's a fact."

"Well, if it ain't a fact, then why is it when she's fixing all those ladies hair at the beauty shop do they say, ooh, and aah, and is that so?"

"Cade," Emma said as she dug her bare toes into the squishy mud, "do you want to do the dare or not?"

"I'm not a scaredy cat, if that's what you are asking."

Emma stood and slowly pulled her string out of the hole. She wrapped her hands around the back of the crawdad to release it's claw's grip from the bacon.

"Darn it. We forgot our bucket." Emma eased the little critter back down into his home.

"We'll come back tomorrow." Cade announced as he pulled his empty string up.

The five o'clock train whistle blew in the distance.

"It's time to go anyways. Get back Emma." Cade instructed as he grabbed Emma's hand and pulled her down into the ditch below the railway.

The ground trembled as the train grew near.

Clang - Clang- Clang.

"Tomorrow instead of fishing, we can do the dare." Emma hollered.

"I can't hear you." Cade shouted.

"I said," Emma began to holler again.

Rumble- rumble- rumble-silence.

Cade stepped over to the tracks and picked up the two pennies.

"I said that we can do our dare tomorrow instead of fishing."

"Flat as a pancake." Cade handed Emma a penny and whistled.

"What do you say Cade?"

"I say I'd probably rather be this penny than do that dumb dare." Cade took off his red baseball cap and put his penny in the secret pocket inside. "But I'm not scared." He said as he put his cap on.

Chapter 9

The weathered house, sat at the dead end of the street, unwelcoming anyone who passed by.

The white paint had long ago chipped to a dull grey, exposing only splinters of the hue that it once had been. The shutters that did remain hung carelessly to one side.

Bermuda grass grew thick across the lawn with yellow dandelions poking their heads about.

"By the time we get to his house, we will be eaten clear up to our necks by red bugs." Cade stated as he handed Emma the binoculars so she could see for herself.

They had found the perfect hiding spot, Mrs. Kitty's flower garden sat at an angle from the old house.

"You have tried to get out of this all morning Cade. We gotta go before Mrs. Kitty gets home and finds us squishing her flowers."

Emma ran out to the end of the street to meet her fate. Cade followed hesitantly behind.

Once they reached the lattice of the porch, Cade cried, "See I am not scared." He then turned to run back.

"Wait! We need a souvenir."

"For what Emma?"

"No one will believe us if we don't have proof."

"You are crazy, Emma."

The lattice noisily popped as Emma pried the board from the house.

"Umph." The ground caught her as she fell back.

As soon as Cade heard the thundering footsteps from inside the house, he ran as fast as he could back to Mrs. Kitty's flower garden. Emma scurried underneath the opening of Mr. Mack's porch.

"Who's under my porch? Come out you scoundrel!" Mr. Mack called.

Emma, sweating and shaking, crawled into the damp, dark coolness under the house. Emma tried not to vision the snakes and rats that would abide here. She clenched as she felt Mr. Mack's hand tightly grasp around her foot. No matter how hard she crawled forward, her body pulled back toward the opening of the porch.

"Now I've got you, you little..." Mr. Mack stopped as he glared down at the mischief maker, "girl?"

Emma held her head down to the ground as she bit her lip so it would not tremble. The dirt shuffled back and forth between her tennis shoes as she tried to determine if she should stand still or run for cover.

"What's your name, young lady?"

"Emma, Emma Richards, sir."

"Emma Richards, huh? Well Emma, why don't you come on in so you can explain to me why it is you are tearing off boards on my house."

Emma's life flashed before her eyes. "I- I- my mother is waiting for me to..."

"Come on Emma." Mr. Mack lead her to the front door. The door slammed behind her. Miserable darkness fell upon Emma pushing out any hope of sunlight.

Chapter 10

"Lawd a mercy, boy. What you be doin' sleepin' in my garden? You smushin' all my flowers all laid up on em like that. Go on, get up." Mrs. Kitty demanded as she nubbed Cade with her foot.

Cade awkwardly stood up trying to make sense of his surroundings. Then he remembered.

"Oh Mrs. Kitty, you gotta help me! Old Mean Mack has Emma. I was hiding out so he wouldn't find me. I was watching for her from here to make sure he didn't hurt her."

"You didn't look like you be watchin' to me, those eyes all closed."

"Well, I got tired I guess."

"Why ya'll be pesterin' that poor old man fer? Ain't ya'll got better things to do?"

"It was Emma's dumb dare. Now he's done kidnapped her. I bet he has cut off her fingers and toes, and I bet he has her tied up with her mouth taped so she won't holler. That's why we can't hear her."

"That's enough child! Your imagination done went and ran off. You come hep me get my groceries in so they won't ruin from this heat, then we can get her."

"Do we have to go down there? He may kidnap us too. We need to call the police."

"We ain't callin no police. Mr. Mack is a fine old man that just happens to like to keep to himself. You call the police and they's likely to arrest you two fer trespassin, seein that's the only crime committed here."

"I guess you are right, Mrs. Kitty."

"I know I be right. Now you go on and get yourself a grocery bag. I don't want my pork chops to be spoilin."

"Mrs. Kitty, why do folks call you Mrs. Kitty for?" Cade asked as the door slammed behind them.

Chapter 11

Emma's eyes squinted shut as they tried to adjust to the dark, dismal room. She couldn't seem to make out the objects that surrounded her.

Mr. Mack led her to the sofa and offered her a seat as he turned on a lamp. Dust flew out of the soft cushion of the couch when Emma sat, causing her to sneeze.

Emma rubbed her knees nervously. Mr. Mack sat across from her watching her sternly.

"O-kay, Emma Richards, explain why you were tearing my property up."

"I-I, well, uh," as hard as Emma tried to speak, she could merely mutter.

"Well, spit it out girl! Why were you vandalizing my property?"

"It was a dare. I am sorry Old Mean Mack, I mean Mr. Mack, sir." Emma sat up attentive and alert. Fear fluttered through her stomach making Emma feel as though she would be sick.

"Old Mean Mack, huh?" Mr. Mack slacked back in his chair. The snarl erased off of his face.

Emma watched his every move without blinking.

If only I would listen to my momma, Emma thought, *If I were more like Kate, I would not be sitting here right now!*

"Is that what they call me child?" Mr. Mack laughed with a tired chuckle.

"Yes sir." Emma replied.

Mr. Mack slowly stood up and walked over to Emma. He peered down upon her, his arm stretched out offering Emma a wrinkled hand. Emma, not knowing what to do, scrunched back into the sofa.

"It's alright child, I am not going to hurt you."

Emma hesitated, then held out a small, naive hand out to Mr. Mack.

"I have avoided this for many years." Tears surfaced in Mr. Mack's eyes as he led Emma to the fireplace mantel. "I guess it is time that I finally let go."

"I will tell you a tale, a true tale, that may explain to you and your friends. Maybe then you will understand why you think of me as mean."

Emma stood silently trying to swallow, but her mouth was dry.

"The day I speak of occurred thirty years ago, December of '47 to be exact. I have not spoken of the day since, but I think of it with every breath that I take."

Mr. Mack reached up to the wooden mantle and took down the dusty frame that encased Maddy's picture.

"This," he held for Emma to see, "is, was, my precious Maddy, Madison Grace."

Emma looked into the eyes of a small child who appeared to be about her age. A generous smile reflected from the innocent face.

"Go on," Mr. Mack insisted. "You can hold it."

Emma's hands wrapped around the cool metal of the frame. A warm sensation ran through Emma's fingertips. The frame slipped from Emma's shocked fingers. She quickly knelt down to retrieve the frame. "I'm sorry."

Emma held the cool frame in her hands once more deciding that the warm, gentle tingle that she had felt was merely her imagination.

Looking into the picture once again, she met questioning eyes that were masked behind the smile. *Why hadn't I noticed them before?* She wondered as she handed the picture back to Mr. Mack.

Those eyes, *three, four, shut the door...*

a faint childlike whisper hummed in Emma's ear. Emma looked around her, but no child was to be found. Her grasp held tightly around the frame.

Emma was startled when Mr. Mack spoke up. "You can let it go child, you won't drop it again.

It was apparent to Emma that Mr. Mack hadn't heard the voice.

Emma let go and watched as he placed the picture back upon the mantle.

Next to the picture sat a pair of tattered red shoes. Emma noticed the scuff marks as Mr. Mack lowered the shoes for her to see.

"These shoes," Mr. Mack choked on the words that he tried to speak, "these shoes, I bought for my Maddy's tenth birthday, the day that she died. She was hit by a train."

Emma stayed silent, though her mind screamed. She herself was ten, Maddy's age. How could a life end so young? And why was this man telling her all of this, this that seemed so important. No grown up had ever talked to her, only told her what to do, when to do it, or how. She was always messing up, and now here is Mr. Mack talking to her, almost like a friend. All she knew to do was to listen.

"Go on, you can try them on. They should fit. You seem to be about the same size as Maddy was."

Emma took her shoes off hoping to get this over with. *This man isn't mean, he's crazy!* Emma thought as she slipped her foot into the patent shoe. The leather, hardened with age, comfortably fit Emma's form. Her eyes met Mr. Mack's as he handed her the other shoe.

Emma offered him a sympathetic smile as she unbuckled the shoe she was wearing.

"Would you, please Emma. It would be wonderful to hear these shoes pitter pat once more."

Emma took the other shoe and slipped it on as well. She nervously shuffled her feet back and forth. A single tear touched the toe of one of the shoes as Mr. Mack looked down.

Emma began to dance as she was overtaken by a sudden inner joy. Laughing gaily, she took Mr. Mack's hand and spun around the dark room. Never had Emma felt so alive. Then she stopped.

"What is it child?" Mr. Mack questioned.

Silence fell upon them. Emma then turned and walked where her feet led.

"Where are you going?" Mr. Mack called, but Emma had no idea herself, so she didn't answer.

She came to the end of the hallway and wrapped her hand around the cold, brass doorknob. Mr. Mack felt torn. "I haven't opened this door since, since…"

"Since the accident." Emma finished for him. She took his hand and placed under hers and together they twisted the knob. The door opened and an array of sunlight fell heavily upon them.

Maddy's red patent shoes pitter pattered as Emma walked around the room wondering what drew her here.

Papa, Papa. The words echoed.

Emma looked up at Mr. Mack to see if he had heard these words as well.

Mr. Mack stood by the door facing in tears.

"Don't you hear her, Mr. Mack?" Emma asked. She had never believed in ghosts, but surely her mind wouldn't be playing this cruel of a trick.

"Hear who, child?"

Emma reached down and picked up a crystal heart from the midst of shattered glass on the hardwood floor. She held it up and the sunlight filled through the glass casting a prism of colors around the room. Music, Emma could hear music.

Papa,

Emma led Mr. Mack into his daughter's room.

"Close your eyes, Mr. Mack and listen. Listen and feel."Emma instructed, not thinking of where she gained this courage.

Papa, Papa, the words echoed.

"Maddy!" Peace washed across Mr. Mack's face.

Papa, dance with me.

The music, the voice, the prism of colors all spun across the room with Emma and Mr. Mack as together they danced.

Chapter 12

The brown paper bags rustled as Cade took out the gallon of 2% milk and the package of pork chops.

Mrs. Kitty opened the gold refrigerator door.

"Go on boy, set them right in here." She pointed to a space in between the bowl of ripe, red strawberries and the tub of butter.

Out of the smaller sack, Mrs. Kitty took a carton of Grade A eggs and a loaf of wheat bread. She put the eggs in the side door of the refrigerator, and placed the wheat bread in the maple wood bread box that sat upon the green kitchen counter.

Cade felt smothered by sunflowers. Mrs. Kitty's kitchen decor consisted of a sunflower salt and pepper shakers, sunflower dish towels, sunflower pictures, sunflower table mats, and even a sunflower fly swatter.

Mrs. Kitty took the brown paper sacks and fold them each along the crease to make them flat. She them slid them with her other paper sacks between the refrigerator and the cabinet.

"Now child, let's go get Emma."

As they walked down the steps of Mrs. Kitty's back door, Cade found the courage to ask again.

"Is Mrs. Kitty your real name?"

"No child, it ain't. My real name be Diedre Jo Nelson, my maiden name Brown."

"Well, why do folks call you Mrs. Kitty then?"

"Kitty be the nick name my deceased husband called me years ago. Everyone began to call me Mrs. Kitty after awhile. I reckon some people don't know that ain't my name. I never thought about it."

"Your deceased husband, what does that mean?" Cade asked, forgetting the nervousness of asking about her name.

"Deceased mean he's dead." Mrs. Kitty replied.

"Well, how did this husband die?" Cade questioned.

"You shore be a nosy one," Mrs. Kitty chuckled, "but I reckon I can tell you. He was kilt in 1953. Three white men murdered him."

Cade's wide eyes urged Mrs. Kitty to continue her story.

"It was our weddin anniversary. Preston wanted to do somethin special, a picnic in the park. I fried up some chicken and put on my best cotton dress. We sat and ate lunch on a blue blanket. We talked, that man shore loved to talk."

Cade kicked a rock as they walked down the road.

"Dark clouds began to cover the sky, so I packed up the wicker basket and we started to walk home. It began to rain so hard that my cotton dress clung to me."

Cade kept quite as Mrs. Kitty told the story.

"Preston said we needed to take a short cut, this short cut led us to white folks territory. I's scared, but walked right beside Preston thinkin he be strong enough to whip ten, folks if need be. I wish I were right."

Mrs. Kitty fell silent.

"Then what happened?" Cade prodded.

"Three white men were standing under an awning of a building. They hollered as we walked by. They say they didn't take to no nigger folk walkin on their street."

"Did Preston hit them then?" Cade asked.

"No child, Preston kept quite and pulled me close. He walked so fast I could hardly keep up. Those white folk walked behind us throwing rocks and calling us nasty names not fit for your ears to hear."

"Then what?" Cade could hardly stand the suspense.

"They trapped us in a alley. Two beat Preston with a baseball bat while another held me to watch. They then strung up my Preston and hung him right there. Then they beat me within an inch of my life for the color of my skin."

"Who called the police?"

"Child, back then the police didn't do nothin for crime against a black man. It was a white man's world. Shore they had to investigate, but it turn's out that one of the men that done it was a nephew to the police chief. Ain't no justice ever been served."

"That's a sad story." Cade said, as they stepped on Mr. Mack's lawn.

"Son, if there's one lesson to be learnt from that story, that be no man should judge another. Each man, regardless of color of skin, has a life. A life to live. Those white men took Preston's life because of their thoughts of what be right. Their prejudices kilt him and robbed me of many memories."

"I bet you miss him."

"I shore do child. That's why I like being called Mrs. Kitty. He gave me that special name, and that's somethin that noone can take from me."

Mrs. Kitty knocked on the wooden door. She then looked down at Cade and placed her hand on his head.

"Names are special, especially nicknames. Generally someone gives a name because of something important. In my case, Preston called me Kitty. It made me feel needed and loved."

Cade smiled. How naive he was to have thought that she was called Mrs. Kitty for having a million cats. Now he knew.

Chapter 13

Mrs. Kitty and Cade stood on the front porch of Mr. Mack's home waiting for him to open the door. No one came.

Mrs. Kitty knocked harder.

"Hello." She sang out as she turned the doorknob and pushed the door open.

She and Cade entered the dark living room.

"Anyone home?" She hollered.

Rustling noises came from the hallway. Finally Mr. Mack and Emma approached.

Emma was pale. Her limbs were sore. Exhaustion overtook her as she tried to walk.

Mr. Mack led her to the sofa.

"Why child, what happened to you?" Mrs. Kitty questioned, as she kept an accusing eye on Mr. Mack. She had always assumed that he was a good man, but didn't actually know firsthand.

"I'm fine, Mrs. Kitty." Emma's words slurred as they fell from her lips.

Mr. Mack brought Emma a glass of ice water. The water was cold and refreshing to Emma's parched throat.

"I should explain." Mr. Mack spoke.

"No sir," Mrs. Kitty replied, "I believe it be Emma that needs to be explainin.'"

Emma sat her glass down on the table beside her. "I met Maddy." She then lay her head back on the sofa and closed her eyes.

Cade sat down beside Emma and held her clammy hand.

Mrs. Kitty turned to Mr. Mack not understanding what Emma was telling her. She remembered the tale of Maddy, but she was confused in how Emma could have met her.

"She's telling the truth." Mr. Mack confessed.

"I have never believed in the spirit world, but Emma somehow contacted my Maddy."

Mrs. Kitty looked around for signs of a ghost, flying furniture, rattling chains, spooky sounds, but the house was silent.

"Well, I best be gettin this girl home. I's sorry they pestered you today." Mrs. Kitty stated as she bent down and lifted Emma up from the sofa.

Mr. Mack seemed troubled. "Please believe me. I meant no harm."

With Mrs. Kitty holding one arm, and Cade the other, they were able to support Emma to walk without falling.

"She didn't pester me," Mr. Mack said, "she brought me peace. Peace that I haven't had in thirty years."

Mrs. Kitty almost felt compassion for the man, seeing the tears that fell from his eyes.

Mrs. Kitty looked back over her shoulder when they had made it to Emma's yard. She could see Mr. Mack's form fading into darkness.

Chapter 14

Mrs. Kitty rang the doorbell of Emma's home.
Jolynn's merry voice could be heard behind the door. "Just a minute."

The doorknob turned and Jolynn's pleasantness subsided when she saw Emma's state. "My goodness, what has happened to her?"

Mrs. Kitty and Cade led Emma into the clean scented home.

"Her room is down the hall."Jolynn instructed. "Let's get her to bed, then we can discuss what has happened."

The coolness of the clean sheets welcomed Emma to rest peacefully as she gave into her fatigue. Jolynn kissed Emma on the cheek, then turned and walked out motioning for Mrs. Kitty and Cade to follow.

When they reached the living room, Jolynn offered her visitors a seat. She thought she had better sit herself to refrain her emotions.

"Now, please tell me what is wrong with Emma."

"Well ma'am," Mrs. Kitty began, "She and this young un here had a dare to go to that Mr. Mack's house, they heard the tales about him bein crazy an all."

"And you let them!"

"Now hold on just a minute! I's ain't let them do a darn thing." Mrs. Kitty protested. "This boy here was hidin out in my flower garden is why I's involved in this here deal."

"Cade is this true?" Jolynn turned to face him.

"Yes ma'am." Cade admitted.

"You doubtin' me ma'am?" Mrs. Kitty accused.

"Yes, no, well I don't know. What did he do to her?"

"Well, he says that your Emma called up a ghost, his daughter, if I recollect correctly, was hit by a train thirty years ago."

"This is nonsense!"

"Yes, I agree. Now if you don't mind, I's need to be goin. I's got a house of my own to clean and some pork chops to be cookin." Mrs. Kitty stood and walked to the door. "I can let myself out."

Jolynn walked behind Mrs. Kitty and felt the coldness in her tone. "I thank you for being so kind to bring her home to me. I'm sorry if I offended you."

"No offense takin ma'am. I's understand you bein upset." Mrs. Kitty smiled and walked away.

Jolynn face Cade. "Now tell me Cade Allan, what are you two doing keeping company with that Negro?"

Cade was dumbfounded. He never guessed Jolynn to be prejudice.

"And why on earth did you dare my daughter to go to that insane man's house? She could have been killed!"

Cade didn't try to correct Jolynn that it had been Emma's dare.

"Here I am at home thinking that you two are out playing like you should why all the while you are up to no good!"

"Can I see Emma, Mrs. Richards?" Cade asked, hoping to be released from Jolynn's outburst.

"No Cade, I believe you have seen enough of Emma today. You best be going home."Cade wouldn't have hurt anymore had Jolynn slapped him.

He walked out to the porch, then turned back to Jolynn's threatening gaze. "Mrs. Richard's, that negro's name is Mrs. Kitty," Cade offered with pride, now knowing the reasoning of her name. "If you would only listen."

"I am through listening Cade. Go on home now, you hear." Jolynn shut the door and locked it behind her.

Chapter 15

Emma tossed and turned rousing from her deep sleep. Ping -ping, she could hear thinking that her imagination was getting the best of her.

Ping - ping, again. Emma sat up and bed and realized that the sound was pebbles hitting her window.

She dropped her legs on the side of the bed letting them dangle for a moment, not trusting them to stand.

Ping - ping, more impatiently. Emma pulled the string of the venetian blind to see Cade standing there eager to speak.

"Emma," she could hear him whisper her name as she lifted the glass window.

"What in the world are you doing at my window like this, and why are you whispering?" Emma demanded.

"Your momma isn't too happy with me."

"That's ridiculous! Why is she mad at you?"

"Well, me and Mrs. Kitty, which I found out why her name is Mrs. Kitty, brought you home from that crazy man's house. What did he do to you Emma? You were sick."

"First things first Cade, why is she called Mrs. Kitty?"

"Well, I wish it was because she liked cats, but it ain't. Some prejudice white men hung her husband and beat her. Kitty is what he called her."

"Well, that's awful. How can somebody not like somebody that they don't even know?"

"Ask your momma, she knows."

"What's that suppose to mean."

"Just what I said, that's why she's mad at me. She said we shouldn't be playing at a "negro's" house."

"That's crazy Cade. She talks to that black boy at Mr. Druther's grocery store all the time, she even tips him a dollar or two."

"That's different. She's o-kay talking to him because he is working for her like a slave."

"You take that back Cade! My momma ain't prejudice. At least she doesn't flap at the mouth like your momma does at that beauty shop. She's always into everybody's business."

Emma was shaking she was so upset. Her face was flushed.

Jolynn swung open the bedroom door. "Emma, who are you hollering"– she went to the window and looked out.

Noone was to be found. "Was that Cade at your window?"

"Yes ma'am." Emma said hoarsely.

"I don't want you messing with him, that negro lady, or that crazy old man again! Do you understand me?"

"Yes ma'am" Emma repeated, realizing that Cade had been right.

"I don't feel good, I am going to lay back down if you don't mind." Emma crawled back into her warm bed and contemplated on how she could again reach Maddy.

Chapter 16

Jolynn had spent the past hour engaging in an uncontrollable cleaning frenzy. Anger twisted in her mind as she polished. Rage vented as she swept the floor. Wrath was thought upon as she unloaded the portable dishwasher. Finally, fury was released by the lulling hum of her vacuum cleaner.

Jolynn pushed the off switch of the vacuum with the toe of her leather shoe. She wound the cord nice and tight around the two pegs that stretched out on the neck of the vacuum.

She stood and inspected her immaculate lemon scented abode. Content with the cleanliness, she wheeled the squeaky vacuum to the utility closet.

Jolynn walked back into the living area and sat down on the welcoming sofa. She lay her head back on the fluffy taupe headrest and allowed herself to rest. She felt spent, numb from limb to limb.

Tick-tock, she heard the clock. Tick-tock, tick-tock. Silence fell upon the room as a black hovering shroud. Something did not feel right.

Jolynn had been taking captive by her compulsion to clean. Anxiety had tormented her mind so that she had forgotten to check on Emma.

She jumped up and ran frantically down the hall and entered Emma's room. Her heart rate eased when she viewed Emma's bed and found the soft form with the covers tightly snug.

No wonder, Jolynn thought. *Silence is from Emma sleeping.*

Jolynn turned to walk away. A bird began to chirp, sounding as though he were in the room. Jolynn tiptoed across the bedroom and pulled the curtain back only to reveal the open window.

The fresh summer breeze slapped Jolynn in the face. She yanked the comforter of Emma's bed back and found neatly arranged pillows that gave the illusion to a body form.

Jolynn's anger returned full force, but this time a cleaning frenzy will not subdue her anguish. She will take action and put her emotions into motion.

"Mom, I home!" Jolynn heard Kate's voice sing out from the kitchen.

Chapter 17

Emma rapped quickly on the door. Her heart thumped in her throat from running so fast.

"Mr. Mack," her voice trembled as she called out.

"It's me, Emma." she added as she let herself in.

"I don't have much time," she hollered out. "My momma will be, Mr. Mack?"

Emma's eyes adjusted to the motionless form that lay peacefully upon the couch.

Emma's fingers fumbled trying to turn the table lamp on.

Light fell upon Mr. Mack. His eyes remained closed and still.

In Mr. Mack's hands, he held a box. Upon the box was an envelope. *To: Emma Richards.*

"Oh," she gasped as she took the box. His hands fell limp by his sides.

Emma then noticed the empty pill bottle that lay upon the table by the lamp.

"Oh Mr. Mack! What have you done?"

Emma bent down and kissed Mr. Mack gently on his cheek.

A faint lullaby hummed in the background. As Emma rose up and looked around it were as though she were on an extravagant carousel. The music roared loudly as vibrant colors of the rainbow danced around and around the room.

She then could hear a child's laughter, and following that was a robust chuckle of a man.

As sudden as the image began, it stopped. Emma's eyes squinted as she turned back to face the body that had imprisoned Mr. Mack for so many years.

In death he may live. Where this thought came from, Emma did not know. She grabbed the box and ran as fast as she could to her bedroom window and climbed in. She carefully hid the box under her bed and hid herself under her blankets.

She had once again found Maddy.

Chapter 18

K ate, put down your things and come with me." Jolynn insisted.
"What is going on?" Kate implored as she obediently placed
her piano books down on the kitchen table.

"There's no time to tell you now, just follow me." Jolynn raced
across the lawn with Kate on her shoe heels.

Jolynn stomped upon Mrs. Kitty's front porch and banged with all
of her might.

"Do we even know this woman, Momma?"

"Enough with all of the questions..." Jolynn began, but Mrs. Kitty
opened the door interrupting her sentence.

"Where is my daughter, you, you, you black varment?"

"Well, you white lady, I's don't know wheres you child be, but she
sho nuff ain't here." Cade stepped out from behind Mrs. Kitty.

"Where is she Cade?" Jolynn demanded.

"Momma, calm down!" Kate pleaded, embarrassed by her
mother's demeanor.

"You tell me where my child is, do you hear me!"

"I's say you child ain't here, ma'am! Now if you'd please get your
white butt off of my black property, I's got pork chops I's be fryin.
I's ain't about to burn em fer a rude, prejudice, no count white
varment like you!"

The door slammed in Jolynn's face.

"Well, I have never!" Jolynn exclaimed.

"You were rude to her," Kate added, "I don't blame her one bit."

Chapter 19

Tap- tap- tap.

"Oh, it's you white folks again!" Mrs. Kitty snarled when she opened the and found who her visitor was.

"Ma'am, I apologize for my mother's behavior." Kate stated.

"We have searched the whole neighborhood for my sister and we haven't found her yet."

"Like I's been sayin, she ain't here."

"I believe that ma'am, but do you or Cade have any idea of where she may be?"

"Uh-uh, and that boy ran off after you two left."

"Oh dear." Kate sighed as she looked around hoping that Emma would jump out from behind a bush to end a silly game.

Jolynn approached the side of the house. She looked stricken.

"Mrs. Kitty," Jolynn wailed, "please help me find my baby!"

"How many times do I's has to tell you, that child ain't here."

Jolynn placed her face in her hands and wept.

Mrs. Kitty sympathized, for she too had felt the pain of losing a loved one.

"Now lady," Mrs. Kitty began,"I ain't one to be gettin off in white folks business, but you's keep puttin me in it, so I's guess I's can says what I think."

Jolynn wiped her eyes and looked up to Mrs. Kitty.

"If it be my child a missin, I'd be a lookin at Mr. Mack's. She seemed mighty curious of that man earlier."

"Oh Katie, that's it!" Jolynn said.

"Thank you Mrs. Kitty. Let's go momma."

"No, wait Kate. Mrs. Kitty, would you be so kind to go with us? I don't know that man."

"Well, I's don't know him either."

"Please, Mrs. Kitty, for me?" Jolynn begged.

"I's guess I's can, but not for you. I be goin for that child's sake."

"God bless you Mrs. Kitty."

"God's already blessed me a plenty. I's don't needs no blessins from a prejudice white folk."

Mrs. Kitty led the way a she mumbled under her breath about smushed flowers, burnt pork chops, and white folks who can't keep up with their children. "Lawd hep me through this day!"

Chapter 20

The three ladies stood on Mr. Mack's front porch waiting for him to open the door.

Six knocks, no answer.

Ten knocks, no answer.

"I know he's here!" Jolynn insisted. "The man never leaves his house."

Twelve more desperate knocks.

"Well, what now?" Kate asked.

Mrs. Kitty turned the doorknob. "I reckon we let ourselves in, that be what."

The lamp was still glowing as Emma had left it. The pill bottle too, remained as it was. The only thing different in the room was Mr. Mack. His form lay as motionless as before, but now there was a hint of a smile upon his face.

"Oh, Lawd a mercy!" Mrs. Kitty shrieked.

Jolynn fell faint.

Kate knelt beside her mother and tried to lift her up.

"She be fine, child! Go, fetch a doctor!" Mrs. Kitty pointed to the green rotary telephone. She then brought her finger down to Mr. Mack's neck hoping to feel a pulse.

Jolynn sat up and looked around. "Kate, help me please. Get momma a wet towel."

"No you don't, child!" Mrs. Kitty demanded. "You white folk pulled me into this here mess, and I ain't about to let you make this about you!"Mrs. Kitty heaved with anger.

"You's get off yo white fanny and hep me with this man, you hear!?!"

"I hear." Jolynn stood up.

Fifteen minutes later, an ambulance roared in front of the house.

Mr. Mack was pronounced dead on the scene due to self affliction.

Mrs. Kitty shook her head with pity as she, Kate, and Jolynn walked home.

Jolynn and Kate entered their yard. Mrs. Kitty continued walking.

"Hey," Jolynn called out, "I still haven't found Emma. Won't you please come in?"

"I will make coffee." Jolynn added.

"Well, I's reckon that be just fine." Mrs. Kitty said.

"I's drink my coffee black." Mrs. Kitty chuckled as she followed them to their front door.

Chapter 21

The aroma of fresh ground coffee filled the kitchen. Jolynn offered Mrs. Kitty the first cup.

"Thank you, ma'am." Hot steam swirled above the dark beverage.

Kate sliced lemon pound cake and served it on her momma's fine china.

"That be just fine." Mrs. Kitty proclaimed.

"Why, thank you. I made this cake from scratch." Kate boasted with pride.

"Child, I mean this plate, but the cake be mighty fine too."

All three ladies supped their coffee and ate the cake as they talked of what they should do next in order to find Emma.

"Daddy!" Kate shouted when the door opened and Jarrett Richards stepped in from work.

A startled expression crossed his face when he eyed Mrs. Kitty sitting at his dinner table eating off of his wife's fine china.

"I am Jarrett Richards. How do you do?" Jarrett offered as he extended his hand to Mrs. Kitty's chubby hand.

"I's be Mrs. Kitty, sir. I's be just fine. It's your wife yous need to be askin though."

"Jolynn?" Jarrett became concerned.

"Emma's gone!" Jolynn dropped her fork on her plate and began to sob.

Jarrett's temper soared. "What do you mean, gone?"

"I mean that she climbed out of her bedroom window and ran away."

"For God's creation! Our daughter is missing, and you three are having a damn tea party!"

"It's coffee, Daddy." Kate corrected, only to get a snarl from her daddy.

"Sir, we's be a lookin fer your child all day. She's bound to come home before dark."

"Have you contacted the authorities?" Jarrett asked.

"No, but I have you to know that we searched this whole neighborhood." Jolynn explained.

"We even went to that crazy man's house that Emma went to, but he was dead." Kate added, trying to help.

"Dead?" Jarrett's fear intensified.

"He kilt himself, sir."

"You have some explaining to do, Jolynn!" Jarrett hollered.

"What's wrong, Daddy?" All eyes turned and focused on Emma. Her hair was tousled, her eyes were swollen. She had apparently been asleep.

"Where have you been?" Jolynn demanded.

"In bed where you told me to be." Emma replied.

"Lawd a mercy lady. You had me all over this neighborhood lookin fer a child that was asleep in they bed?"

"But she wasn't!" Jolynn insisted.

"Well enough." Jarrett said. "At least she is home and safe. That is all that matters." He wrapped his strong arms around Emma.

"Here, have some cake." Kate offered.

Emma sat down in the kitchen chair. She ate her cake in silence.

Emma had always been told that it was rude to talk with her mouth full, so she ate and ate.

Everyone was impatiently waiting. That was everyone except for Kate. She was pleased that Emma liked her cake so much.

Emma was just happy that Kate had given her an escape from speaking.

"Well, I's best be going. It'll be gettin dark soon." Mrs. Kitty said as she stood to pick up her cup and plate.

Jolynn's hand extended to touch Mrs. Kitty's. "I'll get those, and I will walk you to the door.

"Thank you, ma'am." Mrs. Kitty said.

"No, thank you. Mrs. Kitty," Jolynn began. She turned to look at Jarrett in shame, then turned to face Mrs. Kitty, "I apologize for all of the nasty things I said to you earlier. You are a fine, fine woman."

"Well, you's be a fine woman too, Mrs. Richards, for a white folk." She chuckled as she turned and walked across the lawn.

Chapter 22

Emma had only been to one funeral in her life, but she had been only eight months old and did not remember attending.

Her Papa Pete's shirt sleeve had gotten caught on a tractor auger. His field hand had worked frantically to free him, but the machine was much to powerful and quick. Papa Pete had been twisted into his tragic destiny within a matter of minutes.

Emma only remembers the event because of the stories that were passed down. She did not remember the angelic hymns, nor the preacher's monotone sermon. She definitely did not remember having to wear such an awful itchy dress.

She shuffled anxiously back and forth as a small group of people gathered around Mr. Mack's casket.

"Our lives are but a breath…" the preacher said.

Cade stepped up to stand beside Emma.

"Hey," he whispered, "How about going crawdad fishing after this?"

"My mother said I can't play with, OUCH!" Emma's voice announced much louder than her previous whisper. She rubbed her arm where her mother had pinched her.

"Let us reflect on Mack Murray's life, shall we? Anyone?," the preacher invited.

Silence fell upon the group. Emma looked around.

One particular man that seemed familiar to Emma cleared his throat. He was a clean cut man that looked to be in his late thirties. Again he cleared his throat as if he wanted to speak, but instead he would choke up and swallow his words.

"Alright," the preacher began, "If there is noone, the let's proceed."

"Wait!" An elderly man sitting in a wheel chair spoke up. He inhaled as if each breath were precious, exhaling slowly and speaking as loudly as his fragile voice would allow.

"My name," the man said, "is Mr. Wright, Jack Wright. Mack Murray was employed at my lumberyard in the forties. We would all tremble around this man." Jack snickered at his recollection.

"He was tough as an old boot. He wouldn't back down from an alligator if he'd ever meet up with one, or that was what we all thought."Jack's toned softened.

"Some of you may not remember that he had a daughter, I can't remember her name. Anyways, the point is she was ran over by a damned old train." Jack gave his voice a rest, then continued.

"I was the one who found that little girl. I thought it was my duty to tell Mr. Mack. I have been haunted by this ever since. Not only by that poor child, but for this tough man. He crumbled right before my eyes."Again, Jack paused, then continued.

"Why do I tell each of you this?" He questioned.

"I know that Mack kept to himself after this happened. He had no friends in his good days, so I know that noone here would completely understand him taking his own life." Jack looked around and inhaled.

"Mack Murray quit living the day his wife and son walked out on him, the same day that his daughter was hit by that blasted train. Don't judge him, lest ye be." Jack began to cough frantically. He had to refrain from the rest of his speech.

Emma noticed that the familiar looking clean cut man wiped tears from his eyes as he walked away.

"Thank you, Mr. Wright." The preacher said.

"With that being said, let us leave here today with a new understanding of Mack Murray. Let us now sing, Amazing Grace."

Part III

Chapter 23

October 1985

D *ear Emma,*
You are making it hard on me to keep our relationship silent. I wanted to punch Adam when I saw you with him at the football game Friday night! Why are you doing this to me? I feel like I am in elementary school having to sneak you these letters in your locker like this.
Love,
Cade

Dear Cade,
You know you are the only one for me. I had to go out with Adam so my mother will not become suspicious of us. You know how she feels. She won't let the past go. I am sorry.
I love you,
Emma

Dear Emma,
Next week is homecoming. I guess I am going to have to set and watch you flaunt a mum from Adam. I am really getting tired of your mother. I am leaving for UTA at the end of summer. It is hard for me to leave you. I love you Emma, damn do I love you.
Cade

Dear Cade,

I have been trying to put your leaving in the back of my mind. I pretend that it is not going to happen, but it is. What's going to happen to us Cade? If my mother finds out about us, she will send me back to that shrink doctor. I can't go back.

Hugs & Kisses,
Emma

Dear Emma,

One date is all I ask. One real evening with my girl before I have to leave. It is killing me to think that Adam is getting the kisses that are meant for me! As far as to what happens to us, that is left up to you. I don't see much for us since we never get to be together. As far as that shrink, Emma that was years ago. It is water under the bridge. We need to move on. It was a dumb dare that we should have never done. I hate that man killed himself, but it was not your fault. I love you, Emma. Do this for me, PLEASE.

One date...I double dare you!!

Love,
Cade

Dear Cade,

Alright, you have won me over. I have always been a sucker for a dare. I have to go to the game with Adam because that will be my way to get out of the house. Meet me after the game is over at the flagpole in front of the school. That will give us at least two hours before my curfew. I love you too, Cade.

Dear Emma,

I hated to see Friday night end. I have to admit, it was tough during the game to watch Adam with you. I wondered if you would actually go through with meeting me. I think he's falling for you Emma.

The night was much more than I imagined it would be. I only meant to hold you and kiss you. I know that you were confused after it happened, but I do love you. I know we should have waited until after we are married, but it was still special being that it was both of our first time.

I can now leave for college knowing that my girl will be waiting for me. I love you Emma. Now more than ever. Please, let's tell your mom.

> *Love,*
> *Cade*

Dear Emma,

Why are you avoiding me? I thought everything was finally working for us?

> *Love,*
> *Cade*

Dear Emma,

Please answer my letters. I need to hear from you. I would call, but I know that would upset you.

> *Cade*

Dear Emma,

If this is about Friday night, I am sorry. Please, can we at least be friends?

> *Love, Cade*

Dear Emma,

Forget about your mom! Answer this letter or I am coming over!

> *Cade*

Emma,

O-kay, three weeks is long enough. What is going on here? I have the right to know why you have decided to hate me. Meet me after school, or I intend to come to your house. The choice is yours. I love you even if you are stubborn.

> *Love, Cade*

Dear Cade,

I will meet you!! Do not come to my house!

> *Emma*

Chapter 24

Cade waited impatiently in the school parking lot for Emma. He knew that she would wait until everyone left. She wouldn't want anyone would notice them together.

He tapped his fingers on the hard steering wheel of his 79' Ford pickup truck. Subconsciously, he was keeping the beat to a song that blared out from his speakers.

Twenty minutes passed. He started his ignition.

Five more minutes passed. He shifted his truck into second gear and began to drive away. A horn beeped behind him.

Cade looked in his rearview mirror to see Emma's tan hatchback car. His aggravation eased.

Cade then turned his truck off and stepped out to meet Emma. She motioned for him to get in.

Cade opened the passenger door and sat down on the blue leather seat. He noticed immediately that Emma had been crying.

"What is wrong?"

"Just shut the door."

The door slammed. He then turned to face Emma.

Silence lingered, but only for a moment.

"What have I done, Emma?"

"I am sorry, Cade."

"Why are you avoiding me? I know that what we did could have pushed you away, but I love you!"

"Cade, at first it was because you were pushing me to tell my mother about us."

"I love you, damn it! I am sorry that I want the world to know that."

"I love you, too."

"Then what is the problem. There is more to this than your mother."

"You are right." Emma began to sob frantically.

Cade wrapped his arm around Emma and pulled her to him. She pulled back and wiped her eyes.

"What is it? Why do you pull away from me?"

"Cade, I am pregnant, alright! Now are you happy?"

Taken aback, Cade refrained himself.

"Why haven't you told me this?"

"All I hear about is you going to college. Your future is ahead of you. Leave it to me to go and screw it up."

"Emma, you didn't do this. We did. Maybe you aren't."

"Wishful thinking, huh? I've taken three tests. All are positive."

"Well, now we have to talk to your mother."

"No, we do not!"

"Emma, us you can keep a secret, but please tell me how you hide the fact that you will be having a baby, our baby?"

"I may not be."

"What do you mean?"

"Just what I said. I will take it away. I will go on with my life, and you can go to college, as planned."

"I can't believe you! That is my baby, too. I have a say so!"

"This is my body, and my life!"

"You are afraid, damn you!"

Tears streamed down Emma's face.

"What are you afraid of? Why can't you let me love you?"

"It's my mother, alright."

"Here we go again!"

"Yes Cade, here we go again! I have been a constant screw up while Kate has made exceptional grades, the captain of the drill team, the head cheerleader, the president, not to include the volunteer work that she has done. Now, she is attending college.

I on the other hand have eked by in grades, even in photography which I enjoy. My highschool graduation, which hopefully I reach this year, I will be pregnant. What a wonderful daughter! I will make my parents proud."

"Forget Kate, Emma. You are not her. You are you."

"Now you have finally figured it out. I am not my sister, that is why my mother and I do not get along."

Cade felt the pressure intense in his brain. He massaged his forehead with his fingertips.

"You forced me into telling you Cade. I wasn't going to let you know."

"For the last time, this is my problem, or should I say inconvenience, too. I will just postpone college for awhile and take on a full time job. I want this baby."

"That's not fair. I don't intend to have it."

Cade opened the door and stood on the pavement. "I will meet you at your house. We will talk about this there."

"No you don't Cade!"

"I am, Emma! I love you, doesn't that mean anything? Or will your mother always call the shots for us?"

Emma's face took on a sturdy form. She had a thought. Cade could tell when her mind was at work.

"Alright. Go on, Cade. Let's go to my house then."

Cade looked at her and shrugged. He closed her door and got back into his truck. He started the ignition, shifted into second gear and began to slowly drive.

Looking back in his rearview mirror, he could see Emma. She had gotten out of her car and opened her trunk. She had a box in hand. It was to far for Cade to recognize what it was. Emma got back into her car and drove towards Cade. Content that she was following, Cade began to drive away.

Chapter 25

Emma drove close behind Cade assuring herself that she could not be seen in his rearview mirror. Confident that she was following, Cade continued forward to Emma's house. She took a quick right when he least expected it.

Emma continued quickly driving, then took a left, and then another right to throw him off her path if he would have suspected her not following him.

She glanced at her watch, 4:30 pm. She then looked at her fuel tank, which was three quarters full. She then turned on her heater to take out the chill. Coldness, or nervousness, she couldn't tell which, was making her shiver.

Finally, Emma made it to the freeway. She now began to relax and hum to the music from her stereo.

Driving felt good. She went with the tempo, the flow of the traffic, and the destination of her heart.

All her life she had done what others had expected of her, now it was her turn to pay back the promise that she made to Mr. Mack many years ago. It was all wrong, but it felt at the moment so right.

Going to Kansas was on impulse, true, but it had been a trip often thought of, but seemed impossible until now. How much more could she screw up? She would not go home until this "baby" issue was resolved, and Kansas would give her a place to go until then.

Emma wiped warm tears away from her face. She continued to drive putting miles and miles between her and the ones that she had let down. Thoughts to turn around came, but only for a moment. She pushed them aside, knowing that in reality she could never return.

Chapter 26

Jolynn was standing on the front porch beating out a rug when Cade turned into the driveway.

"Hello," Cade said as he approached her. He felt uneasy that Emma had not turned in behind him. He had assumed that she was right behind him.

"Hello, Cade." Jolynn said, wiping the sweat from her brow.

"What brings you here, Cade?"

"Actually, Emma, but she apparently didn't follow me like she said?"

"Cade, not to offend you, but you do realize that I prohibit Emma from being with you. You two seem to get into trouble."

"No offense taken," Cade said smugly, "but I am not as bad as you make me out to be."

"That's for me to judge, now why don't you run on along home. I don't want you boggling Emma's mind on that mess of the past. She has finally gotten over that spell. I don't want any relapses."

"No offense to you ma'am, but you make your daughter sound like she is a mental case."

"It is no concern to you on how I refer to my daughter. Now run on along as I have said or I shall beat this rug out on your head rather than my porch!"

"Yes ma'am." Cade agreed realizing why Emma ran rather than following him to her home.

He shook his head. "I will call on her later."

"That will not be necessary, Cade." Jolynn quickly responded.

"Oh, it is more than necessary." Cade then started up his truck and drove away.

Chapter 27

Emma hesitated on calling home collect, but after six times calling Cade at home, she knew where he was.

"Hello!" Jolynn's voice was short and raspy.

"Hi, mom."

"Where in hades are you? It is two o'clock in the morning?"

"Please don't holler at me."

"Don't holler! Your dad has to get up in three hours to go to work, we are all worried sick!"

"Is Cade there?" Emma asked ready to hang up if he wasn't.

"Yes, he does happen to be here. I called him at ten when you hadn't came home."

"Can I speak to him please?"

"I don't think so, Emma! You run away every time you have something to do with him."

"That's not fair, Mom! Either I talk to him, or I hang up this phone!"

Emma heard the phone slam down. Seconds later, Cade responded.

"Emma! You have scared us. Where are you?"

"Have you told them anything?"

"No, why?"

"Well, I have made up my mind, Cade. I am scared about this baby thing. I can't do it alone."

"I told you, I will help. You won't be alone."

"No, I mean that I am scared to terminate it alone. Please come with me. Don't let my parents know, or I will never be able to come back home."

"Are you crazy!" Cade replied, noting that everyone's eyes were on him.

"Do you realize what you are asking?" Cade calmly asked.

"Yes, I do."

"Where are you Emma?"

" I have made it to Ardmore, Oklahoma."

"Where exactly are you going?"

"I am going to Topeka, Kansas Cade. I thought you might come along."

"Why there, Emma?"

"To bury an old ghost. Do you want to or not?" Cade then remembered the battered box she had taken out of the trunk of the car.

"You are running, Emma!"

"I take that as you don't want me to wait for you."

"What about the other issue?" Cade carefully selected his words in front of her parents.

"I need to do this Cade! Just forget it! I will do this all by myself!"

The phone clicked. Emma had hung up and he wasn't exactly sure where she was.

"Where is she?" Her father asked.

Cade glared at Jolynn. His breath was heavy and deep. Cade ran out to his truck offering not an explanation to any one. He started his truck and headed towards Ardmore.

"God, Please don't let her do anything stupid until I get to her!" Cade prayed out loud as he sped away.

Chapter 28

Sunlight peeped into the windshield of Emma's car rousing her from a restless sleep. She rubbed her swollen eyes and stretched out her arms. An uncontrollable shiver overtook her limbs. It was so cold.

Emma started her car. She shifted the gear into drive, and immediately remembered why she had to pull over to sleep in the first place. Thump- thump. Emma pulled back onto the shoulder again.

"Darn tire!" Emma had driven all night. After calling Cade, she pressed onward. Her tire blew out around 4:30 am. She was to scared to get out in the dark, and to exhausted to attempt changing a tire. She turned off her ignition and closed her eyes intending to only rest her eyes.

Now, at 6:35 am, the sun had risen, exhaustion had been attended to, but the tire remained flat. Emma beat her hands on the steering wheel and cried.

"Why does everything have to be so complicated?"

She unlocked her door and went to the trunk. She raised it up and unscrewed the handle holding her spare tire. She lifted the tire out of it's compartment and tossed it in the grass. She then took out the jack and walked to the front of the car.

Emma placed the rod into the jack and began to crank. Up, up, it went, slowly lifting her car. "This shouldn't be to hard." Emma thought, then the car slammed back down. It had slipped from the axle.

Emma groaned. She stood up, shivering from the intense cold.

Vehicles passed, but noone offered to stop. She got back into her car to warm up.

Twenty minutes passed, her sitting and thinking. Snow flurries began to fall.

So entranced with the snow, Emma had not realized that a man had approached her window. She jumped back startled. The man stepped back. She wouldn't open her door. He then pointed at her tire.

Emma rolled her window down a bit.

"You have a flat tire."

"Yes sir, I know."

"Would you like for me to change it for you?" the gentleman asked.

Emma looked back and saw that he was driving a red tow truck. She looked at his features, taking them all in. His red and black shirt matched his red and black cap. His brownish beard had been neatly trimmed. His hazel green eyes seemed honest.

Emma gave into the stranger. She opened the door and got out into the boisterous cold.

"Mornin' ma'am, I'm Wade, Wade Granger." He extended a generous hand.

Emma offered him her frigid hand. "I'm Emma, sir."

"Nice to meet you, Emma. This won't take long, but you may want to put on a jacket."

Emma wrapped her arms around herself. "I'm fine."

Wade looked up from the jack. "I saw your plates say Texas. Not as cold down there as here, huh?" He walked to his truck and pulled out a red jacket that had a G emblem on the chest. Granger's Tow Truck Service. Wade offered it to Emma. "It's my wife's, but she won't mind."

Emma gratefully accepted the jacket. "Sir, I only have four dollars. I know that won't be enough."

Wade turned to face Emma. "How old are you, child?"

Emma blushed as she silently avoided the question.

"Well, I am not sure where you are headed, but I do know that traveling alone can be dangerous." Wade took off his cap and handed it to Emma.

"Put this cap on, it will make travelers think that you are a boy."
Wade shook his head and returned to the flat tire. Within minutes, he had the spare tire on and the tools back into the trunk.

Emma held out the four dollars that fluttered from the brisk wind.

Wade waved his hand. "No need for that, this is a courtesy call of kindness."

He then walked to the door and opened it. He glanced down at Emma's fuel tank, which was on the red.

"How far are you going?"

"Topeka, then back to Texas." Emma replied.

Wade shook his head. He looked at Emma. The floppy cap and the oversized jacket, just a child. She reminded him of Sheyla, his sixteen year old daughter. The thought of her traveling alone shook him.

"Have you had breakfast yet?" Wade asked.

"No sir." Emma's stomach had been rumbling, but she had ignored it's insistence.

"Well, there is a café and gas station about a mile or two back up the road. How about I extend my kindness and buy you breakfast and fill your fuel tank up before you go?"

The relief that came upon Emma's face pleased Wade.

"I will take that smile as a yes. Follow me."

Emma turned her car and followed Wade's red tow truck to the café.

"Our angel." She thought aloud, then cringed realizing that she had spoken to her unborn child.

Chapter 29

Cade had driven all night. Emma had not waited in Ardmore, Oklahoma as he had desperately wanted. He frantically drove forward to Topeka, Kansas hoping that he would find her.

He rubbed his eyes pushing back the overwhelming fatigue. He could sleep later. He had to find Emma, and, he choked back tears, his baby.

Cade passed the Kansas State line. In Andover, Kansas, he looked in his rearview mirror to see a highway patrol.

Cade let out an agitated sigh as he pulled his truck to the shoulder.

"You must be in a pretty big hurry, sir." The officer suggested as he took the insurance card and driver's license that Cade offered.

Cade nodded his head. "Yes sir, I am."

"Going 80 in a 65, this ought to be good." The officer rested his arms on Cade's open window giving him 'all attention' to his reason to speed.

"I have driven all night from Texas, headed to Topeka. My girlfriend has ran away."

"Topeka, Kansas, huh? That's my hometown. Where, specifically, would she be headed to in Topeka?"

"I am not sure. A farm of some sort. She, we knew a man, that died years ago. He left her a box of their dead daughter's belongings. He asked if she would someday return it to his wife and son that had left him."

"What's the name? I know about all the farms in Topeka."

"Mack Murray was the man's name."

"Murray, nope, doesn't ring a bell."

"Emma mentioned Patsy, maybe Patricia, was the wife's name. Willie, I believe, was the boy's."

"Sullivan's place, I bet. Is the lady older?"

"Yes, she would be older."

"Mrs. Sullivan, she has a son named Willie. He's a little older than me." The patrolman offered.

"What is your girlfriend's name, and what does she drive?"

"Emma Richards, a tan, hatchback car. I don't know the model."

"Yes," the officer said on his radio, "Has anyone pulled over an Emma Richards, driving a tan hatchback, model unknown?"

Cade could hear static, then a female voice registering in the frequency waves. "I have an Emma, unsure of last name, driving a tan car, license number RN 325 I, Texas plates. Possible runaway, turned in by Wade Granger, tow truck driver, who stopped to change a flat this morning. She was headed to Topeka."

"She is about two and a half hours ahead of you." The officer said as he turned from his radio. "My son was a ranch hand on that farm until her son returned and took over management. The farm is not hard to find, but I bet you would be wasting time if you go straight there. My boy said that her son, Willie, came back and tossed her butt into the nursing home before anyone could blink an eye. Twilight Tower's, I believe, is the name of it. Downtown Topeka. You can't miss it. Get going so you can find her."

"Thank's officer."

"No problem."

"Sir, you forgot about my ticket." Cade stated.

"No I haven't, just be careful not to get stopped again."

"Thank you, sir."

"Good luck." The officer nodded as he walked away.

"I will need it." Cade thought feeling a bit more positive now that he knew a direction to go in.

Chapter 30

The snow was steadily falling as Emma drove into Topeka. She had the heater on as high as it would go.

She reached down onto the passenger seat and unwrapped the sausage and biscuit that Wade insisted that she take with her. Thankful that he did, she ate not wasting a crumb.

She opened her soda and drank. The fizzy caffeine lingered on her tongue.

She put the drink bottle in the holder and tossed the empty wrapper on the floor.

Emma then pulled off onto the shoulder of the highway. She opened the glove compartment and pulled out the envelope and the cardboard box.

She had often anticipated this visit. It almost seemed unreal that she was finally holding up to her promise to Mr. Mack and Maddy.

"At least I will please someone." Emma said aloud as she took note of the address that Mr. Mack had written inside.

Emma started back onto the highway and took the turn on the gravel road that the letter had directed.

Snow made the road slick, so Emma drove at a snail's pace.

Time seemed to stand still.

She thought of Maddy, and imagined the woman that she would have been. The letter didn't explain much, except that her mother had went away. Emma would give her the items in the box, but what would that resolve? It wouldn't bring her daughter back.

Emma took a right turn on a desolate lane. The battered mailbox slanted to one side. Emma stopped, unsure if this was the right place.

She read the directions again.

It seemed to be right.

Upon the hill, she could see a white farm house. She drove forward.

Emma noticed a man working on a fence in the meadow. She pulled into the driveway and turned off her ignition.

The man turned back and looked at her. She recognized him immediately. He was the same man that had attended Mr. Mack's funeral years ago.

She walked up to him holding the box and envelope in one hand, and extending the other to shake his hand.

His puzzled expression stumbled Emma. She lowered her hand.

"My name is Emma. I promised Mr. Mack that I would bring these things to uh," she looked at the envelope, "Patricia and Willie."

"Mack's been dead along time, now run along." He shooed at Emma.

Emma turned to walk away, defeated. She thought of Maddy, then turned back.

Willie had began to work on the fence again.

"I have driven from Texas, ran away from my family, to keep a promise that I made to Mack the day he died. It has taken me all of these years to get the courage to do this, so the least you can do is tell me where your mother is if you are not interested." Willie continued to work, ignoring her presence.

"I am not leaving until you hear me out!" Emma demanded.

Willie looked at her. "You are a persistent one. Mother's not here, you will find her at the nursing home, Twilight Towers, room 109. She doesn't talk much anymore though, so don't get your hopes up. She only grunts noises."

"You will go with me," Emma insisted, "I promised to tell both of you."

Willie threw his fencing tool down and walked over to Emma.

He wiped his sleeves over his eyes. As cold as it was, Emma knew that it was tears instead of sweat that he was wiping away.

"Yes, I'll go. I would like to see what the old man had to say."

"That's settled then. We can go in my car since it is already warm."

85

Chapter 31

Emma and Willie entered the front glass doors of the retirement center. The sterile room was quite, although there were several tenants sitting around.

A man in a wheel chair reached out to Emma as she walked by. She stopped to acknowledge him.

Willie shook his head. "She's this way, if you want to see her."

"I think you got your bitterness from your father," Emma complained. "He wasn't always so friendly either."

Willie snarled. "Let's just get this over with please."

"Wait," Emma said, startled.

"Now what?!"

"Cade!" Emma ran to the nurses station. Cade had just about given up hope in finding her.

He ran to Emma and hugged her. "You have everyone worried."

"Cade, this is Mack's son, Willie. Willie, my friend, Cade."

Willie again avoided handshakes.

"Come with us, Cade. I am giving Patricia Maddy's things."

Cade pulled Emma aside. Willie continued to walk to his mother's room.

"Emma, this is foolish. We are going home."

Emma pulled her arm from Cade. "This is something that everyone has told me is crazy, but what I have wanted to do for years. Me, Cade. I want it. Foolish is me thinking that you would come this far to support a decision that I have made."

"I came this far because of the decision you are making about our baby."

Emma glared at Cade. She turned and left him standing.

The door to room 109 stood slightly ajar. She could here a voice moaning. She peeped in to see Willie holding Maddy's red patent shoes. His eyes were red.

Emma approached him and placed her hand on his shoulder. She then walked over to Patricia. "Patricia,"

"She can't understand," Willie interrupted.

"But she deserves to hear." Emma continued as Cade walked in.

"My name is Emma Richards. I met Mack, and in some sense I met Maddy, years ago. I do not understand what Mr. Mack wanted in requesting me to bring these things to you, but maybe you will. I made him a promise, so here it is."

The frail form lay in the bed. Her gray hair matted to the form of the pillow. Her eyes were shallow. Her mouth was a hollow form.

Emma took the black and white picture of Maddy out and placed it in Patricia's soft hands. Patricia's eyes ventured back and forth.

Emma then took out the heart shaped trinket that was all that had remained from the shattered music box on Maddy's floor. She placed the heart in Patricia's other hand.

Willie held tightly onto the red patent shoes, so Emma didn't attempt to take them away.

"What happened? I never knew?" Willie's voice trembled.

"I don't know all of the story," Emma offered, feeling Cade's presence beside her. "I was only ten. Mr. Mack only told me that you and your mother left, and that Maddy was hit by a train."

"M-M-Maddy," Patricia's voice formed.

"I- I will tell you of M-Maddy."

Willie ran over to his mother, for she hadn't spoken in years.

"Your father and I," her weak eyes searched for Willie. "fell in love when I was fifteen. Oh, was that man a gentleman."

Patricia took a deep breath, and continued. "I found out I was with child. I left the farm to marry your father. I was afraid of your Grandma and Papa finding out, so I ran. I was a child, afraid. Then, it was too late. We left. Maddy was ran over by a train."

Patricia sobbed as though years of grief was trying to be released.

"By that time, Papa had died of pneumonia, but Momma was still alive. Mack sent us letters of Maddy, but I had to deny her and act like he was a drunkard. Momma would have been to upset to know that I had been with child before I married. I resented Mack all those years for taking me away, but it was my fault for not telling my Momma in the first place. My whole life, wasted."

Emma felt Cade's hand tighten upon her shoulder.

Emma knelt down to Patricia, tears fell from her eyes.

"Ma'am, I am running from my family, I am with child."

Patricia lay the heart down on the blue blanket and grasped Emma's hand.

"Child, turn back. Don't run as I have. I can't change my past mistakes. I can only pray that God doesn't deny me as I did my Madison Grace."

Emma stood and turned to Cade. "I am ready to go home now."

Willie stood wiping his eyes. "I will need a ride home if you won't mind."

Cade took Emma's key off of her chain and tossed it to Willie.

"Take her car, I am not letting this girl out of my sight."

Emma turned to Patricia, then to Willie. "I thought you would be thanking me, but instead I thank you."

She and Cade walked out of the retirement center hand in hand.

Epilogue

D on't this beat all?" Mrs. Kitty proclaimed as she held the bundle of baby in her arms.

"Mrs. Kitty," Emma began, as she lifted herself up in the hospital bed.

"Yes, child," Mrs. Kitty answered, not taking her eyes off of the baby girl.

"Cade and I have been wondering," Emma reached over to take Cade's hand for support, "why did you not ever have any children."

Mrs. Kitty looked up with a sad expression on her face.

"Me and Preston, we wanted a babe so bad. We's tried, but I never did. He always say, "That's alright, Kitty," but I's know in his heart he wanted a babe. That man was sho nuff good to me, I's know he'd make a fine daddy."

"Did you ever get upset because you never had any?" Emma asked.

"Yes child, but one thing I learnt in life is God knows best. I reckon he know that my Preston was gonna be kilt and I would've been left to raise a youngun on my own."

"Emma and I would like for you to be our baby's Godgrandmother."

"Oh," Mrs. Kitty held Madison close, "You hear that Preston, we's are grandparents."

Then, as quick as her smile came, it faded.

"What yall's folks gonna think about this" They may not want this child to a black folk Mawma Kitty."

Emma courageously spoke. "This is our decision, as husband and wife."

"So that is that." Cade proudly stated.

"Well, that be mighty fine, mighty fine." Mrs. Kitty began to hum softly gently lulling Maddy to sleep.

KANSAS– EMPIRE GAZETTE

OBITUARIES…SEPTEMBER 28, 1986
PATRICIA ANN SULLIVAN PASSED AWAY PEACEFULLY TODAY AT THE TWILIGHTS TOWERS NURSING HOME. SHE HAS ONE SON, JOHN WILLIE MURRAY, OF TOPEKA, KANSAS. FUNERAL ARRANGEMENTS HAVE BEEN MADE AT CASTON'S FUNERAL HOME. SERVICES WILL BE AT 2:00 PM SATURDAY. BURIAL WILL BE IN TEXAS, SO SHE CAN REST IN PEACE BY HER HUSBAND MACK, AND DAUGHTER MADDY. MAY THEY WELCOME HER WITH OPEN ARMS.

TEXAS- DAILY CHRONICLE

BIRTH ANNOUNCEMENTS…SEPTEMBER 28, 1986
CADE ALLAN AND EMMA LOUISE STEPHENS ARE PROUD TO ANNOUNCE THE ARRIVAL OF THEIR BABY GIRL, MADISON GRACE STEPHENS, 8LBS. 2OZ, 21IN. MAY SHE ALWAYS DANCE IN THE MEMORY OF MADDY.

Printed in the United States
30087LVS00006B/25